THE LAST OF THE MOHICANS

JAMES FENIMORE COOPER

SADDLEBACK
EDUCATIONAL PUBLISHING

Saddleback's *Illustrated Classics*™

SADDLEBACK
EDUCATIONAL PUBLISHING
www.sdlback.com

ISBN-13: 978-1-56254-918-3
ISBN-10: 1-56254-918-9
eBook: 978-1-60291-158-1

Printed in Guangzhou, China
0310/03-68-10

13 12 11 10   3 4 5 6 7 8 9

Welcome to
Saddleback's *Illustrated Classics*™

We are proud to welcome you to Saddleback's *Illustrated Classics*™. Saddleback's *Illustrated Classics*™ was designed specifically for the classroom to introduce readers to many of the great classics in literature. Each text, written and adapted by teachers and researchers, has been edited using the Dale-Chall vocabulary system. In addition, much time and effort has been spent to ensure that these high-interest stories retain all of the excitement, intrigue, and adventure of the original books.

With these graphically *Illustrated Classics*™, you learn what happens in the story in a number of different ways. One way is by reading the words a character says. Another way is by looking at the drawings of the character. The artist can tell you what kind of person a character is and what he or she is thinking or feeling.

This series will help you to develop confidence and a sense of accomplishment as you finish each novel. The stories in Saddleback's *Illustrated Classics*™ are fun to read. And remember, fun motivates!

Overview

Everyone deserves to read the best literature our language has to offer. Saddleback's *Illustrated Classics*™ was designed to acquaint readers with the most famous stories from the world's greatest authors, while teaching essential skills. You will learn how to:

• Establish a purpose for reading
• Use prior knowledge
• Evaluate your reading
• Listen to the language as it is written
• Extend literary and language appreciation through discussion and
  writing activities

Reading is one of the most important skills you will ever learn. It provides the key to all kinds of information. By reading the *Illustrated Classics*™, you will develop confidence and the self-satisfaction that comes from accomplishment—a solid foundation for any reader.

Step-By-Step

The following is a simple guide to using and enjoying each of your *Illustrated Classics*™. To maximize your use of the learning activities provided, we suggest that you follow these steps:

1. ***Listen!*** We suggest that you listen to the read-along. (At this time, please ignore the beeps.) You will enjoy this wonderfully dramatized presentation.

2. ***Pre-reading Activities.*** After listening to the audio presentation, the pre-reading activities in the Activity Book prepare you for reading the story by setting the scene, introducing more difficult vocabulary words, and providing some short exercises.

3. ***Reading Activities.*** Now turn to the "While you are reading" portion of the Activity Book, which directs you to make a list of story-related facts. Read-along while listening to the audio presentation. (This time pay attention to the beeps, as they indicate when each page should be turned.)

4. ***Post-reading Activities.*** You have successfully read the story and listened to the audio presentation. Now answer the multiple-choice questions and other activities in the Activity Book.

Remember,

"Today's readers are tomorrow's leaders."

James Fenimore Cooper

James Fenimore Cooper, the son of a wealthy politician and landowner who founded the frontier village of Cooperstown, New York, was born in Burlington, New Jersey, in 1789. He studied at Yale for a few years, but left the university to sail aboard a merchant ship. In 1808 he became a midshipman in the U.S. Navy. The career, too, was cut short in 1811, when he left the Navy and was married.

Soon after marriage he began writing the five frontier adventure novels which were later to become known as *The Leatherstocking Tales*. They are: *The Pioneers*, *The Last of the Mohicans*, *The Prairie*, *The Pathfinders,* and *The Deerslayer*. His hero and main character, Natty Bumppo, called Hawkeye in *The Last of the Mohicans*, was a perfect example of the backwoodsman: honest, hardworking, noble, and a friend to peaceful Indians.

Cooper's novels have been translated into many languages and have enjoyed great popularity because of their vigor and adventure. Cooper himself was pleased with his work and continued to write into his sixties. He died in Cooperstown, New York, in 1851.

Saddleback's *Illustrated Classics*™

THE LAST OF THE MOHICANS

JAMES FENIMORE COOPER

Uncas

Hawkeye

Chingachgook

Cora Munro

Magua

Alice Munro

David Gamut

Duncan Heyward

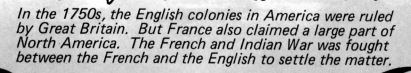

In the 1750s, the English colonies in America were ruled by Great Britain. But France also claimed a large part of North America. The French and Indian War was fought between the French and the English to settle the matter.

Some Indian tribes sided with the French, others with the English. Much of the fighting took place in the land that was to become New York State.

One summer evening, an Indian runner brought an important message to the British Fort Edward by the Hudson River.

8

Soon after dawn the next day, 1,500 troops set out on the road to Fort William Henry.

Later a smaller group left Fort Edward to go to Fort William Henry.

Who are the important-looking people?

General Munro's daughters who go to join him. The officer travels with them.

Cora and Alice Munro, with Major Duncan Heyward, began their journey of some twenty miles through the forest. The Indian runner Magua would show them the way.

This is the trail.

But do we not follow the troops down the road they took? Is that not safer?

Magua will guide us by a little-known path. It is a shorter and easier way.

But he is an Indian! Can we trust him?

He was once an enemy, Alice, but he is now a friend. If I did not believe so, I would not trust him with your safety!

If there are enemy Indians nearby, they will follow the troops, hoping to pick up scalps. The secret way will be safer!

And it is wrong not to trust the Indian just because his manners are different and his skin dark.

They followed the Indian down the narrow path. Soon they heard another horseman coming up from behind.

What a strange-looking person!

Who is he and what is he doing here?

I hope you don't bring us bad news.

I hear you are riding to Fort William Henry, and I wish to join you.

Who are you, sir? What do you do?

I am a singing master, David Gamut by name!

I am glad to meet you, stranger. Perhaps you and I will enjoy our trip more by singing a duet!

Nothing would give me greater joy than . . .

I must spoil your idea, Alice. To be safe we must travel as quietly as we can. You must put off your singing.

Suddenly Chingachgook bent over until his ear nearly touched the ground.

Listen! White men's horses are coming!

Hawkeye, they are your brothers! Speak to them.

That I will. Here they come. God keep them from the Iroquois.

Friends to the law and to the king. We have traveled all day looking for the crown fort known as William Henry.

Who comes here, among the dangers of the forest?

We trusted an Indian guide to lead us by a shortcut, and now we are lost!

An Indian lost in the woods . . . strange! Is he of the Mohawk tribe?

Not by birth, but adopted by them. He serves with our forces as a friend.

But he fooled you, and then ran away?

Neither, it seems! Here he comes behind us.

Let me look at him! If he is a true Iroquois, I can tell by his sneaky look and by his paint.

Silently, the scout went back to look at Magua. Hawkeye saw that he was Le Renard Subtil, *an Indian working for the French who had given him that name.*

Le Renard *had led Heyward into a trap. Hawkeye, Heyward, and the Mohicans tried to capture him, but the crafty Magua escaped into the forest. It was almost night.*

We must follow him! We are four strong men to one!

He would bring us within range of his friends in a minute! Unless we move and throw them off our trail, our scalps will hang before Montcalm's tent tomorrow!

Do not leave us! Stay and help me defend the ladies!

You are right. It would not be the act of real men to leave such harmless beings to their fate! We will do what we can, if you will promise two things.

Name them!

You must be as still as these sleeping woods, no matter what happens. And you must never tell anyone about the hiding place where we take you!

We will do our best.

Then follow me! We are losing time!

While the Indian led the horses away to hide them, Hawkeye drew a bark canoe from its hiding place. He told Alice and Cora to get in.

Hawkeye's expert paddle moved the canoe upstream against the current. Almost afraid to breathe, Cora and Alice watched as the rapids swirled about them.

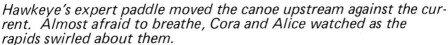

They drew near to a great waterfall. Alice hid her eyes, sure the canoe would be tipped over.

A last move by Hawkeye and the canoe floated, still, beside a low, flat rock.

At the foot of Glenn's Falls. Climb onto the rock, and I will bring the others.

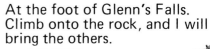

In seconds, the girls and Heyward were safe on the big rock. The canoe shot away downstream.

Almost before they could believe it, the canoe had returned with the rest of the group. Hawkeye and his Indian friends showed them the secret of their hiding place.

Where the rock is softer, the water has worn it away. We are on an island of rock, with the falls on two sides of us, and the river above and below!

Wonderful! And it seems very safe!

But is there no danger of surprise? A single armed man at the entrance could hold us at his mercy.

Such old foxes as Chingachgook and I are not caught in burrows with only one hole! The cave has a second door . . . and beyond is another cave!

Except for the howling of wolves on the river banks, the group spent a peaceful night. Cora and Alice slept soundly on a bed of branches. At daybreak, Hawkeye awakened them.

Now is the time to travel! Be ready to get into the canoe when I bring it. Be silent, but be quick!

Hawkeye went out. Suddenly the noise of yells, cries, and rifle shots broke out all around them.

OH! HELP!

BANG! CRASH! CRACK!

What is it? Can men make sounds like these?

Outside the caves, taking shelter behind the rocks, they were joined by Hawkeye and the Mohicans.

The Iroquois are all around us, on both sides of the river!

Our best chance now is to keep the Indians off the rock until Munro can send a party to help. God grant it may be soon!

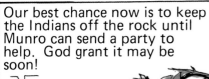

The ladies and Gamut, who has no gun, must return to the cave.

Chingachgook, you and Uncas take posts here where you can see the foot of the falls.

Heyward and I will move upstream where we can guard the head of the island from attack.

In the center of the island grew a few small pine trees. Hawkeye and Heyward hid among the trees and rocks.

It's been a long time. Perhaps they've given up!

You know not the nature of a Huron if you think him so easily beaten back without a scalp. There are forty of them out there, and they know how few we are.

Look! But keep down! They are swimming downstream to our island!

If they miss the island, they will be pulled over the falls!

One of the Indians was swept away, but four others reached the island.

A whistle from Hawkeye brought Uncas to their help. The three stayed down, their guns ready.

They are gathering for their rush. The lead man, at least, will die!

AIEeeeeeeeee!

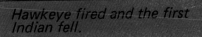

Hawkeye fired and the first Indian fell.

Uncas killed another. Soon Hawkeye and Heyward were fighting hand-to-hand with the others.

Slowly Hawkeye's stronger body won out.

Suddenly he pulled his hand away, and drove his sharp knife into the heart of the Indian.

Meanwhile, Heyward was fighting another warrior.

Both were slipping on the rocks near the falls.

Then, at the last moment, a hand holding a knife appeared over his shoulder.

As Uncas' saving arm pulled Heyward backward, the enemy fell over the cliff.

There was a shout from Hawkeye.

Hide quickly! The work is but half-done!

The other Indians have stopped shooting for fear of hitting their own braves. Now they'll make up for lost time.

Uncas saved my life! He has made a friend who will never need to be reminded of what he has done!

Friends often owe their lives to each other in the forest. Uncas has stood between me and death five times!

The enemy rifles fired, clipping tree branches and nicking rocks.

Let them use up their powder. We'll use ours only when it counts.

Unseen, an enemy brave climbed a tall tree that leaned toward the island.

Look! Danger!

Killdeer will take care of this one!

That was the last charge in my powder horn and the last bullet in my pouch. Uncas, go to the canoe and bring up the big powder horn.

Uncas slipped away, making his way to the rock where the canoe was tied. Suddenly he shouted. Forgetting danger, they rushed to see what had happened.

The canoe with all our powder! The Iroquois have stolen it!

The three quickest, surest rifles in the woods—and no more use than so many weed stalks.

What will become of us?

It may be a minute, it may be an hour. But the enemy will come, and we will be scalped!

Surely something can be done!

Only prepare to die bravely!

Why die at all, brave men?

We owe you too much already! Surely you can slip away!

The river might carry us beyond the reach of Iroquois rifles . . .

Then go! Why add to the number of the dead?

It is better that a man die at peace with himself than live and be haunted by an act of fear!

Go to our father. If we should be carried into the northern wilds, tell him to rescue us!

There is reason in your words. Chingachgook! Uncas! Hear you the words of this woman?

Hawkeye spoke in their language to Chingachgook and Uncas. The older man listened, nodded. Stepping to the edge of the rock, he dropped into the water and out of sight. Hawkeye prepared to follow.

If you are carried off, try to leave signs to mark your trail

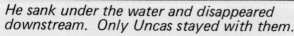

He sank under the water and disappeared downstream. Only Uncas stayed with them.

Your friends are safe. It is time for you to follow.

Uncas will stay.

Go young man, to my father! It is my wish, my prayer that you go!

Uncas' calm face became gloomy, but he followed Cora's command and slipped into the water.

There! He is safe!

Let us hide ourselves in the cave and trust God to help us!

I will hide the entrance.

Suddenly from outside there were fearful whoops and cries. The enemy had reached the island.

Surely, in this hidden spot, we are safe!

They have not found us yet. There is still hope.

Time passed. The cries died away. Then Alice gasped and pointed.

The cruel face of Magua, Le Renard Subtil, *peered into the dark cave.*

With a war whoop, Magua announced what he had found.

WHOooo--- ooo-ooo!

The Englishmen were dragged from their hiding place.

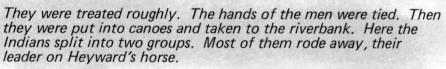

They were treated roughly. The hands of the men were tied. Then they were put into canoes and taken to the riverbank. Here the Indians split into two groups. Most of them rode away, their leader on Heyward's horse.

Six, with Magua as chief, kept watch on the prisoners. With the sisters on horseback, this group set off.

Keep up your courage! All is not lost!

After traveling many miles through the woods, they climbed a steep hill.

Heyward tried to talk to Magua.

General Munro at Fort William Henry will pay well if you return his children safely.

Bring the dark-haired daughter and say Magua wishes to speak!

30

Heyward brought Cora forward.

What would *Le Renard* say to Munro's daughter?

Listen . . . Magua was born a chief and a warrior . . . then he fought for the English under Munro!

Then by Munro's orders he was tied up and whipped . . . leaving these scars!

I think that was for being drunk, which was against the law set by Munro.

The pale-faces brought the firewater! Should they punish the redskin for drinking it?

And therefore would you harm Munro's helpless daughters? At least release my gentle sister!

She can return to the old chief. It is you who must swear to obey!

And what must I promise?

You will follow Magua and live in his tent forever.

The daughter of Munro will draw my water, hoe my corn, and cook my meat.

Monster! I will never do what you say!

Angry, Magua spoke to the other Indians. He talked of their warriors who had been killed. As they listened, their eyes blazed with anger.

Shall we let these people go? Shall we have no white scalps to show for our work?

The warriors dragged the girls away. Others brought ropes and firewood.

32

The Indians fell back, frightened at this sudden death.

La Longue Carabine!

Le Gros Serpent!

Kill the varmints! No one gets away!

Le Cerf Agile!

Soon the battle was ended except for the struggle between Magua and Chingachgook.

Suddenly Magua dropped. He looked lifeless.

Victory to the Mohican!

But as Chingachgook aimed the final blow, Magua suddenly rolled over the cliff. He landed on his feet and leaped for cover.

A sly fox to the last! But he can do no more harm for now . . .

34

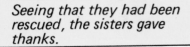
Seeing that they had been rescued, the sisters gave thanks.

We are saved! We will return to the arms of our dear father!

Friend, I thank you that the hairs of my head still grow where they were planted.

It was nothing. It is often seen if you stay long among us!

How is it that we see you so soon, and without help from the fort?

Had we gone to the fort, we would have been too late to save your scalps!

Instead we stayed near, followed, and watched where they took you.

Which was our good fortune!

Soon, with Hawkeye's help, the party set out again through the great forest to find the fort.

After a long and weary journey, stopping only to eat and sleep, the scout led them up a steep trail just after daybreak. From a place on the edge of a cliff, they looked down upon Lake George, Fort William Henry—and the enemy!

We are too late! Montcalm has already filled the woods with his Indians!

The French have begun an attack on the fort!

Surely we can find a way to join our father in his danger!

There is a mist rising from the lake. Perhaps we can slip through the French lines in the fog.

Silently the party crept through the woods in a heavy fog.

Qui va là?

C'est moi . . . ami de la France!

*It was the wrong password. The Frenchman ordered his men to fire.
But suddenly danger came from a new direction.*

Fire, men, fire!

Stand firm, my soldiers! Fire low and sweep the French!

Father! Father! It is I, Alice! Save your daughters!

'Tis she! God has saved my children! Don't fire, men, but drive off the French with your swords!

*Out of the mist to drive away the French came Heyward's own
troops. Following them appeared the figure of the fort's commander,
General Munro.*

For this I thank thee, Lord!

After all their trials, the party had at last reached the safety of Fort William Henry. But the fort itself was in grave danger.

For five days now we've been attacked by Montcalm and his French and Indian troops. It would seem that General Webb and his army have forgotten us.

There is still no word from him?

I hear that Montcalm has captured a messenger carrying a letter from Webb to me.

The walls of the fort are falling. Food is running out.

It is an army I need from Webb, not letters!

Montcalm wanted a meeting with Munro. Heyward went with Munro to speak for him.

I have asked for this meeting to show you that I have more men than you. You have fought bravely, with honor. It is time for you to give up.

38

Sir, you serve the French king well. But the British king, too, has many faithful soldiers.

If you mean General Webb's army, here is his letter.

Webb will send no troops. He advises me to give up!

Sir, we still hold the fort! Let us sell our lives dearly!

Wait! Hear my terms! I will not take your honor away from you!

The fort must be captured, but you may keep your flags.

And guns?

Keep them! None can use them better.

I have seen two things I never expected—an Englishman afraid to support a friend, and a Frenchman too honest to profit from it!

A treaty was drawn up and signed by Munro. It was announced that fighting would stop. The fort would be taken, but the men would keep their guns, their flags, and their baggage. In this way, as army law stated, they had not lost their honor as soldiers.

Montcalm told his Indian friends that peace had been made. They must no longer fight the English troops. One of them was Magua.

Peace? Not a single Indian has a scalp, and the palefaces make friends?

Let Magua prove himself a great chief by teaching his Indians how to act toward our new friends!

Friends? Ha! I will never be friend to him who has beaten me!

On the morning of August 10, the English troops marched out of their fort.

Behind the English troops and wounded came a crowd of women and children following Cora and Alice.

I have no army duties, so I offer you my help!

Thank you, David!

Suddenly the women were attacked by Indian warriors. One reached for the bright shawl in which a mother had wrapped her baby.

Magua appeared and gave a war whoop.

At the sound, 2,000 Indians burst from the forest.

Alice fainted.

Go, save yourself!

No! If the boy David tamed Saul's evil spirit with music, I will try its power here.

David raised his powerful voice in song. Many Indians, admiring his courage, passed by.

How good it is, O see,
And how it pleaseth well,
Together, e'en in unity,
For brethren so to dwell . . .

But Magua, hearing, knew that Alice and Cora were again at his mercy.

Instead, Magua took Alice in his arms and moved swiftly toward the woods.

Come! My tent is still open! Is it not better than this place?

Never! Strike if you will, and kill me!

Stop! Let her go! What do you do?

Wait, Cora!

Knowing that Cora would follow while he held Alice, Magua quickly reached the place where he had horses hidden. Once again the sisters and David found themselves captured by Magua.

Some time later, five sad figures hunted over the scene of the fighting.

Suddenly Uncas pulled from a bush a scrap of Cora's green veil.

We have not found the bodies of Alice and Cora. That is a hopeful sign!

My child! Find my child!

Uncas will try!

Uncas darted away. Deep in the forest he found another scrap of veil—and also a footprint.

Le Renard Subtil—Magua!

That devil again!

Where has he taken my daughters?

By now they are probably near the Canadian border. But what matter? With the Mohicans and me on the trail, we will find them!

Traveling sometimes by canoe, sometimes on foot . . . knowing the trails and the ways of the Indians . . . the Mohicans led the party north. At last they found a strange figure.

Look! An Indian settlement—and one of the Indians!

The "camp" is a colony of beaver! Your Indian is our old friend the singer!

David! You are dressed as an Indian! Where are the ladies?

They have been captured. They are troubled in spirit, but safe in body.

Bless you for those words.

Alice is in this camp. But Cora was sent to a tribe in a nearby valley.

Magua keeps the usual Indian practice of separating those who are captured!

Their souls are softened by song, and I am allowed to come and go at will.

No doubt they think you mad. The Indians never harm a madman!

It would be well for David to return and tell the ladies we are near. When he hears a bird call three times, he can come out to meet us.

Wait! I will go with him!

You! Are you tired of seeing the sun rise and set?

I too can play the madman, the fool. I can be anything to rescue Alice whom I love! I will go with David!

You are brave! Chingachgook has many paints. Sit on the log and he can soon make a fool of you!

With great skill, Chingachgook drew on Heyward's face the lines and colors that meant a friend and a fool.

No warrior marks—only friendship!

Hawkeye gave Heyward much good advice. He arranged for signals and a meeting place. Then Heyward and David left. A half-hour's walk brought them to the Indian camp at dusk.

It is too late to go back. I must not show fear!

The great French king has sent me, who knows the art of healing, to ask if any of his children, the redmen, are sick.

Do the wise men of the Canadas paint their skins?

As an Indian chief lays aside his robe and wears a shirt among his white fathers, so I wear paint among my red brothers.

The chief agreed. Heyward began to breathe more freely. Suddenly a fearful yell sounded from the forest.

Ooowwww—ooowww—oowwoo!

But the Indians were glad.

Ugh!   Good!

It was the return of a war-party. A line of Indians carried scalps. A line of others brought a brave who had been captured.

All at once the young brave, like a deer, leaped over the heads of the other Indians and ran for the woods.

Aieeeeee!

For a moment it seemed he might reach the forest. But the whole group ran before him and drove him back.

Uncas! It's Uncas!

The chief admired the bravery of the Indian who had tried to escape.

Delaware, you have proved yourself a man. Rest in peace till the morning sun.

Suddenly another warrior arrived. Everyone ran to see him. Then Heyward felt a touch on his arm and heard Uncas' voice.

Do not be afraid! Munro and Chingachgook are safe, and Hawkeye's rifle is not asleep! Go . . . we are strangers!

Knowing the danger of their talk, Heyward moved away to look at the newcomer. With great fear, he saw that it was Magua.

So! It is Uncas, who has sent many of our braves to the happy hunting ground!

You must die!

Take him away! Let us see if he can sleep this night, and die in the morning!

Looking for Alice, Heyward circled the camp from hut to hut. But there was no sign of her. At last he returned, hoping to question David.

Here the chief came near to speak to him.

Our French father sends you to help us. That is good! An evil spirit lives in the wife of one of my young men.

Yes?

Can you frighten the spirit away with your skill?

I will try!

The chief led Heyward out. They turned away from the tents and took a path toward the base of a mountain. Suddenly a dark figure arose ahead of them.

A bear! A pet I hope!

Paying no attention to the growling bear, the Indian pushed aside a door in the mountain.

Follow!

Grrr-r-r-r!

Heyward followed, the bear growling at his heels.

Grr-r-r!

48

They came to a large room lighted with torches. David stood nearby.

David! You here?

I am about to try the power of music in healing!

First-born of Egypt, smite did He, of mankind, and of beast also . . .

David left the room, speaking to Heyward as he passed.

As the last notes died away, the two men were startled.

Oooow—oowow . . . owooo . . .

The bear, in a half-growl, seemed to echo David.

She expects you, and is near!

Sending the other woman away, the chief took Heyward to the bedside.

Now let my brother show his power!

Fearful of giving himself away, Heyward prepared to perform. Each time he tried, the bear drove him away.

The spirits are watching! I will go. Do your best for her!

Left alone with the bear, Heyward expected an attack. Instead its head fell to one side and he saw a familiar face.

What has led to this plan?

I will tell you the whole in order . . .

Hawkeye!

Shhh! The varmints are all around!

He told how, having left Munro and Chingachgook safely hidden, he and Uncas had set off to find Cora. They had come upon a party of Huron warriors.

One of them ran away. Uncas ran after him and fell into a trap.

Alas, yes. He has been captured and will die at sunrise!

Having shot a few Hurons, I came in close to the village. There I found a medicine man dressing. A tap on his head, some ropes to tie him to a tree, and here am I in his place!

Now to work! Where is the gentle Alice?

Heaven knows! I have looked in every tent in the village.

The singer said, "She is at hand." There are enough walls here to hide the whole tribe!

A bear should climb. I will take a look.

Shhh! She is there!

The sight of a bear would frighten her!

For that matter, Major, you are a fearful sight yourself! Best wash off that paint!

Good! The path through that door leads to her.

Soon Heyward came to another room.

Alice!

Duncan! I knew you would not leave me!

But you are alone! Is that safe?

With the help of our friend, the scout, we may find our way out of here.

There was a tap on Heyward's shoulder. Turning, he met the evil, laughing face of Magua.

The palefaces trap the beaver. But the redskins know how to trap the palefaces!

Indian, do your worst!

Will you speak those words at the stake while you are being beaten?

The bear appeared in the doorway. Thinking it was the medicine man, Magua paid no attention to it. He went to call in the other Indians.

Fool! Go play with the children and squaws!

Grrrrrr!

Suddenly the animal grabbed Magua in a bear hug.

Heyward rushed forward and tied up Magua's arms.

Magua could only glare as he was safely bound and gagged.

For now the Indian is harmless! We must push for the woods.

Alice has fainted again! Go, friend! Save yourself!

Wrap her in these Indian blankets. Then carry her, and follow me!

They wait outside! Talk to them, Major! Tell them you have shut the evil spirit in the cave, and you carry the woman out!

Outside, the crowd fell back. The chief stepped forward.

Have you driven away the evil spirit? What do you carry?

The evil spirit has been driven out and is shut up in the cave.

I take the woman away, where I will make her better!

Go! I will enter the cave and fight the evil one!

Are you mad? The sickness will enter you. Or you will drive it out and it will enter the woman again! Stay outside, and fight it if it appears!

We will stay!

In the open air, Alice woke up again.

Follow the brook to a waterfall. Climb the hill. You will see the fires of the Delaware Indians. Ask for their help. You will be safe.

Surely we don't leave you here!

The Hurons hold Uncas, the last of the great Mohican blood! I go to see what can be done for him.

54

In his bear costume, Hawkeye found David, who showed him the tent where Uncas was held. Thinking that Hawkeye was an Indian who would torment Uncas, the braves said nothing when he and David entered the tent.

Hawkeye!

Yes, lad! Quick! You will dress as the bear. I will change clothes with David. He will stay here and become you while we escape, since the Indians will not harm him.

The plan was carried out. Uncas and Hawkeye reached the woods safely.

Now let us make our way to the Delaware camp!

But soon the trick was found out. The braves discovered Magua in the cave and cut him loose.

Uncas must die . . . and with him, Hawkeye!

Now all of Magua's prisoners had been set free. He planned to get them back, not by force but by a trick. At dawn he led his braves to the Delaware camp. Seeing them, the Delawares called a meeting.

To speak for the Delawares was Tamenund, an Indian so old and wise it was said that he spoke with the Great Spirit.

What brings you, a Huron, here?

My prisoners are with the Delawares. I come to take them back with me.

The Great Spirit will judge both you and them. Huron, take them and depart!

Quickly the Huron stepped behind Heyward and Hawkeye and bound their arms. Magua lifted Alice in his arms and told the others to follow. But Cora rushed to the feet of Tamenund.

Old one, one of your own people has not been heard. Hear him before letting the Huron depart!

It is an Indian we have captured.

Let him come.

Uncas was led forth. One of the Indians reached for his neck ornament and vest and tore them off.

A tortoise! The sacred blue tortoise!

It was a sign that Uncas was a chief of the oldest and greatest Indian tribe in America. From this tribe the Delawares themselves had come!

Who are you?

Uncas, son of Chingachgook, a son of the great turtle! The blood of the turtle has been in many chiefs, but all others have gone back into the earth.

I thank the Great Spirit that one is here to fill my place! Uncas is found!

Accepted as a great chief of the Delawares, Uncas quickly proved that Magua had no right to keep Hawkeye, Heyward, and Alice.

But Cora was different. Magua had brought her to the Delawares to keep for him. By their law, she was still his.

Mohican, you know that she is mine!

It is so.

You are protected now by our laws, but your path is short! When the sun is above the treetops, men will be on your trail.

At that time, Uncas and Hawkeye led the Delawares on the warpath. They fought a bloody battle with the Hurons near the Huron village.

Driven back, the Hurons made a stand at their meeting tent. Suddenly Magua and another brave broke away

With Uncas and Hawkeye following, Magua entered the cave.

There he goes!

The dark passage going upward seemed to be inside the mountain.

All at once, ahead, they saw three figures against the light.

Have we lost them?

No, I see a white robe ahead!

It's Cora!

Cora! Cora!

Running on, they came out at an opening high on the mountainside. Above, Magua and his men climbed over the rocks.

Stop, dog of a Huron!

Suddenly, on a ledge, Cora stopped.

Kill me if you will, Huron. I will go no farther!

Woman, choose! My tent or my knife!

With a cry, Uncas leaped for the ledge from above.

Uncas!

As Magua fell back, the other brave drove his own knife into Cora.

As Uncas fell between them, Magua drove his knife into Uncas' back.

Uncas rose from the blow, and with his last breath struck down the man who had killed Cora.

Then Uncas faced Magua, who prepared to stab him again.

Magua did so, and Uncas fell dead at his feet. Hawkeye, reaching the ledge across the rocks, gave a wild cry. But Magua leaped away and scrambled for the cliff top.

Stop, you Huron killer!

I leave the paleface dogs on the rocks for the crows!

Suddenly Magua slipped. One of his hands grasped the cliff top.

Slowly he pulled himself up, only a hand grip from safety.

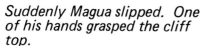

Hawkeye drew his rifle to his shoulder and fired.

Aiieeeeeeeeeeeeeeeeee!

Six Delaware girls sang of the virtues of Cora. They threw sweet-scented flowers and herbs over her body.

The Delawares had won. But the next day's sun rose on a tribe of sad Indians. All gathered to mourn for the dead.

Later, the Delaware girls carried her body to its final resting place.

You have done well. The white man thanks you.

Nearby, the body of Uncas was dressed in the finest robes the tribe could find.

Why do my brothers mourn? The Great Spirit had need of such a brave, and he called Uncas away! As for me, I am a single pine tree in a forest of palefaces. I am alone.

No, no, not alone. Our colors may be different, but we travel in the same path. The boy has left us. But Chingachgook, you are not alone!

The two clasped hands and bowed their heads, their tears watering the grave of Uncas like falling rain.

Then Temenund spoke.

The palefaces are masters of the earth, and the time of the red men has not yet come. My day has been too long. I have lived to see the last brave of the wise race of Mohicans.

And it was many years before the Indians stopped telling of the white maiden and the young Mohican who had gone together to the happy hunting ground.

THE END